OLD WAYS, NEW WAYS

Tana Reiff

A Pacemaker® **HOPES** *And* **DREAMS** Book

GLOBE FEARON
Pearson Learning Group

Old Ways, New Ways

Tana Reiff
AR B.L.: 2.5
Points: 1.0

UG

HOPES *And* DREAMS

Cover photo: The Bettmann Archive, Inc.
Illustration: Tennessee Dixon

ISBN 0-8224-3682-5
Printed in the United States of America

8 9 10 11 12   06 05 04

Globe
Fearon
Pearson Learning Group

1-800-321-3106
www.pearsonlearning.com

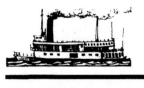

CONTENTS

CHAPTER 1

New York City,
Lower East Side, 1914

Pound, pound, pound.
Solomon Gold
pounded the nail
into the shoe.
His son Sidney
watched him work.

"When does school
start up again?"
asked Sol.

"Next week,"
said Sidney.

"That's good,"
said Sol.
"School is important.
Very important.

I want you
to get good marks.
You are smart.
You work hard,
you'll do fine.
Hand me that shoe,
will you?"

    Sidney handed his father
the shoe.
"How can you do this
day after day?"
the boy asked.

    "What do you mean?"
asked Sol.
"This is my work.
I work hard.
I am a good shoemaker.
I put food
on the table.
Someday
you'll work, too."

    "Not here,"
Sidney said to himself.

"You and I
can work side by side,"
Sol went on.
"We can build
the business together.
Look how far
I have come already!
When I first got
to America,
I worked
in a crowded shop.
I helped to make shoes
for pennies.
Now I have
my own shop."

Sidney looked
around the little room.
Maybe this
was his father's dream.
But Sidney
could never spend
his whole life here.
Helping his father
when school was out
was one thing.

But work here always?
Never!

   "You are only 14,"
said Sol.
"You do not understand
how it was
for your mother and me.
You do not understand
anything about
where we come from."

   "I know
you come from Russia,"
said Sidney.
"You don't speak English.
And you fix shoes."

   "School is very good,"
laughed Sol.
"But it does not teach
some important things
you should know.
Let me tell you
how it was."

Thinking It Over

1. How are Sol and Sidney different from each other?

2. How important is school to you?

3. What important things have you learned outside of school?

CHAPTER 2
Russia, 1882

Solomon Gold
was sleeping.
"Wake up!"
cried Solomon's mother
in the middle
of the night.
"The house
is on fire!"

Young Sol
jumped out of bed.
He felt a blast of heat.
He saw orange flashes.
He ran outside.

Sol heard
his father's voice.
"Stop it!"
cried Sol's father.

Some men with sticks
were beating him.
Some of the men
threw stones.

Sol ran
to his father.
"Stop hurting my father!"
he told the men.
Then Sol was hit
by some stones.
He screamed.

Two big men
pushed the boy away.
Then they all left.
Sol's father
lay in the street.
He was not dead.
But his blood
was all around him.
Sol helped him
to stand up.

Over the next weeks,
Solomon Gold's father

began to feel better.
But he was angry.
"What is going on?"
he cried.
"First they
tell us Jews
that we are not
real Russians.
Then they pass laws.
The new laws say
Jews may not buy land.
And only a few Jews
may go to school.
Then these men
come here to beat and kill.
They burn our house.
Now they tell us
that all Jews must move
to the city!"

"Oh, no!"
said Sol's mother.
"Our family has lived here
for hundreds of years!
We never made
any trouble."

Even so,
the family
had to leave their home.
They went
to a city
in the west
of Russia.
All the Jews
had to live
in one part
of the city.
Most jobs
were closed to them.

"We have taken enough!"
said Sol's father
one day.
"We cannot live
like this.
It is too hard
to be Jewish
in Russia.
We must escape
from this country.
We will go
to America."

Thinking It Over

1. Why do you think
   such laws were passed
   against Jews in Russia?

2. What would you do
   if you were a Jew
   in Russia
   in the 1880s?

CHAPTER 3

"So now you know,
my son,"
said Sol.
"And your mother's story
is much like mine.
This is the life
we came from."

Sidney Gold
had heard the story before.

"I am happy
to work hard,"
said Sol.
"Why?
Because here
we can be Jewish.
No one
tells us
we cannot be Jewish.
And here,

you and your sister
can go to school."

Just then
two of Sol's friends
came into the shop.
Sol looked up
at the clock.

"Is it noon already?"
he asked.

"We are early,"
said one of the men.
"We came
to visit
for a few minutes."

Sol's friends
came to the shop
every day.
But today
was Friday.
On Fridays
all the shops
closed early.

All the Jewish men
went to pray and sing.

"Are you coming along?"
Sol asked Sidney.

"Of course,"
said Sidney.
The boy
locked the back door.
He closed
the windows.

Sol pounded
the last nail.
"Let's go!"
he said.

They walked
out into the street.
This morning
the street
had been full of people.
Men sold
food and clothes
on the street.

The street was loud
and full of life.
Now the last wagon
was rolling away.

Even the women
had gone back inside.
Sidney's mother, Hannah,
was cooking
special food
for Friday night.

Sidney turned the sign
on the door.
"Closed,"
it read.
But everyone around
knew that already.
It was Friday
in the Lower East Side.
It was not a time
to do business.

Thinking It Over

1. How important
   is religion to you?

2. Do you ever
   eat special foods
   on a special day?

3. Do you believe
   there are times
   when people should not work?

CHAPTER **4**

The Gold family
lived in four rooms.
Sol and Hannah
slept in the living room.
They slept
on folding beds.
Emma, Sidney's sister,
had a small room
off the kitchen.
Sidney shared his room
with a boarder.

The boarder
was not a member
of the family.
He stayed
with the Golds
for a dollar a week.
Having a boarder
helped the Golds
make ends meet.

Each boarder
stayed about a year.
Then another one
would move in.
This week
the old boarder
moved out.

New York
was crowded.
Everyone needed
a place to live.
Hannah had no trouble
finding someone
to share Sidney's room.
When Sol and Sidney
got home,
a new person was there.

"Meet our new boarder,"
said Hannah.
"This is Mr. Fine.
He is a teacher."

Sol and Sidney
shook Mr. Fine's hand.

"Glad to meet you,"
they both said.

Sidney liked Mr. Fine
right away.
But Sol
was not so sure.
Sol did not like
Mr. Fine's looks.
This man
was Jewish.
But he was
a different kind of Jew.
He looked
very American.
And why
had he not been
at a temple today?

To Sidney,
Mr. Fine looked
very interesting.
Sidney wanted
to get to know him better.

Thinking It Over

1. What do you do
   to make ends meet?

2. Why do Sol and Sidney
   see Mr. Fine in different ways?

3. Do you think Mr. Fine
   will be good or bad
   for Sidney?

CHAPTER 5

Mr. Fine
was an English teacher.
He spent
most of his time
at the school.
But many nights
he and Sidney
sat up late.
Mr. Fine
told Sidney
about great books.
They read together.
They talked
about what they read.

Mr. Fine
did not act
like the Jews
Sidney knew.
He did not pray
three times a day.

He did not
take off Friday afternoons.
He went
to a coffeehouse
on Friday nights.
There, he talked
about new ideas.
He came home
very late.

"I think
you spend too much time
with Mr. Fine,"
said Sol.
"You should spend
more time
at the temple."

"I think Mr. Fine is
very interesting,"
said Sidney.
"I want to know
all about him."

One day,
Sol, Hannah, and Emma

were out shopping.
Sidney began
to ask Mr. Fine
some questions.

"My father
has a beard,"
said Sidney.
"Why don't you?
Aren't you Jewish?"

"I am Jewish,"
Mr. Fine explained.
"I am
a new kind of Jew.
We do not believe
in all the old ways."

"Do you eat
Jewish food?"
asked Sidney.

"Not always,"
said Mr. Fine.
"Have you ever

eaten anything
but Jewish food?"

"No,"
said Sidney.
"I may not do that."

"Would you like
to try some?"
asked Mr. Fine.
"It won't hurt you!"

Sidney said yes.
Then he and Mr. Fine
went to a store.
They bought food.
Much of it
was new to Sidney.
They came back
from the store
and cooked
on Hannah's stove.
They sat down
and enjoyed
their meal.

Just then,
Hannah walked in.
"What are you eating?"
she asked.

Sidney told her.
She became
very angry.

"Pig meat!"
Hannah screamed.
"This is not
Jewish food!
You have made
my home unclean!
Mr. Fine,
you must leave!
You put bad ideas
into our boy's head.
My husband and I
won't hear of this!"

Then Sol walked in.
When he saw
what was going on,
he became angry, too.

"Go now!"
he shouted to Mr. Fine.
"Don't you ever
talk to my boy again!"

Mr. Fine stood up.
He picked up
a few things
from the other room.
Then he walked out.

"But, Mother,"
Sidney began.
"Mr. Fine is . . ."

"Not a word!"
said Hannah.
"Go and wash!"

She cleared the dishes
from the table.
She threw them all away.

"That does it!"
said Sol.
"No more boarders!"

Thinking It Over

1. What should parents do
   when they don't like
   their child's friend?

2. What kinds of people
   do you find interesting?

3. Do you think
   Mr. Fine should have cook
   on Hannah's stove?

CHAPTER 6

"So fast
you grow up!"
said Hannah.
She looked
at her children.
Emma was 19 now.
Sidney was 17.
"You are beautiful,
both of you!"

Sidney
had almost finished
high school.
After school
he fixed shoes
with his father.
At night
he went
to Jewish school.
He was learning
the Jewish books.

Pretty Emma Gold
acted in Jewish plays.
She had the lead
in tonight's play.
Her family
would be right there
to watch her.

"I must go now,"
said Emma.
"The lights go down
in two hours.
I can't be late
for makeup.
And don't you
be late either!
I'll be looking
for all three of you!"

After the play,
Hannah, Sol, and Sidney
went to see Emma.

"How did you like
the play?"
Emma asked.

"It was very fine,"
said Sidney.

"You were beautiful,"
said Hannah.

Sol said nothing.
He turned away.

"How about you, Papa?"
Emma asked.
"Didn't you like
the play?"

"It wasn't funny,"
said Sol.

"It wasn't supposed
to be funny,"
said Emma.
"Our plays
are about real life."

"Is that fun,
acting out real life?"
asked Sol.

"Yes, in a way,"
said Emma.
"But I have plans.
I want to act
in other plays, too."

Soon after,
Emma landed
a big part.
The theater
was uptown.
The play
was going to open
on a Friday night.

"You will come
and see me,
won't you?"
asked Emma.

"We cannot come
on a Friday night!"
said Sol.
"You should not
be there either.
Not on a Friday!"

"But this is New York,"
said Emma.
"New York
does not stop
on Friday night!"

"You want
to be rich and famous,"
said Sol.
"But remember,
you are Jewish.
Jews stop
on Friday night.
Friday night
is not the time
to get rich and famous!
I, for one,
will not come to see you
if you act
on a Friday!"

But Emma
went on acting
on Friday nights.
Her father never went
to another play.

Thinking It Over

1. Do you believe
   Sol is being silly
   about Friday nights?

2. Do you believe
   Emma should be in plays
   on Friday nights?

CHAPTER **7**

Sol began
making shoes,
not just fixing them.
He made fine shoes.
He sold them
out of his shop.

"My shoes
are too good
for this little shop,"
Sol told Sidney.
"I am going uptown.
I will sell my shoes
to a big uptown store.
I will get
50 cents a pair!
Just watch me!"

So Sol
tied together
15 pairs of shoes

by their strings.
He hung
the string of shoes
around his neck.
He put on
a funny red hat.

"You are going uptown
looking like that?"
laughed Sidney.

"Yes, I am!"
said Sol.
And out the door
he went.

Sidney put his hands
over his eyes.
He shook
his head.
"My father!"
he said to himself.
"People will think
he is crazy.
They will never
buy his shoes."

Sol walked
30 blocks uptown.
People looked at him.
He kept on walking.
At last,
he reached
the big store.
It was owned
by Jews.

"I make fine shoes,"
he told them.
"I think
your store
should sell my shoes.
Look at the toes.
Nice and round.
Look at the bottoms.
Look inside them.
Did you ever see
such nice shoes?
And smell them!
Smell how fine!
I'll sell you
my handmade shoes
for 75 cents a pair!"

"You are dreaming!"
said the man.
"I'll give you
25 cents."

"Sixty-five,"
said Sol.

"Forty,"
said the man.

"Sixty cents
and no less,"
said Sol.

"Fifty cents
and that's it,"
said the man.

"OK, 50 cents
a pair,"
said Sol.

"And I'll give you
ten cents

for that silly hat!"
added the man.

"The hat's not for sale!"
said Sol.
"People will know me
by my hat!"

Sure enough,
Sol went home
with no shoes
around his neck.
And sure enough,
people got to know him.
The big stores
always knew
when Solomon Gold
was there.
They could spot
that silly red hat
a block away.

Thinking It Over

1. Do you ever
   reach a price
   the way Sol did?

2. People knew Sol
   by his red hat.
   What do people
   know you by?

3. Did you ever feel
   your parents were actin

CHAPTER **8**

Sidney Gold
went on
to City College.
It was free.
His father
wanted him to go.
He lived at home.
As often as he could,
he worked
in the shoe shop.

One summer morning
Sidney asked his father
if they could talk.

"I want you
to understand something,"
Sidney began.
"I plan
to finish college.
But I do not plan

to come back here.
I cannot look at shoes
all my life."

"I do understand,"
said Sol.
"You are
a bright boy.
Your whole life
is in front of you.
You must do
big things!
But I have
an idea, my boy.
We could build
this business!"

"You already have
two other people
working here,"
said Sidney.
"You sell
lots of shoes."

"We should
start a factory,"

said Sol.
"We should make shoes
by the hundreds.
You can learn
how to run a business.
Then we will start
our shoe factory."

"I am not sure
I want to be
in business,"
said Sidney.
"I am not sure
what I want to be.
But I'll think about it."

It was Friday.
It was almost noon.
Sol began
to close up the shop.

"I'll go
to the temple
with you,"
said Sidney.
"But I have plans

for tonight.
I'm going out."

"To see your sister
in some uptown play?"
asked Sol.

"No,"
said Sidney.
"I'm meeting friends
at a coffeehouse.
We get together
and talk there."

"What is wrong
with you young people?"
Sol shouted.
"You are so smart.
But you don't care much
about the Jewish life.
Today is Friday!
This is not the time
for plays and coffee!"

But Sidney
went to the coffeehouse.

It was a dark room
in a basement.
The room
was filled with smoke.
Sidney lit his pipe.

   He talked
with his friends
far into the night.
They talked
about politics.
They talked
about school.
They talked
about books.
They even talked
about Emma's new play.
Sidney enjoyed
this kind of talk.

   He did not want
to face his father
when he got home.
The other young people
had the same problem.

Thinking It Over

1. Do you think
   Sidney has a right
   to go to the coffeehouse?

2. Why is it hard
   for some people
   to decide
   what they want to be?

3. What can happen
   when a child gets educat
   and a parent did not?

CHAPTER 9

College life
was new and different.
There were
many bright people
with new ideas.
Sidney loved it.

Two years
went by quickly.
It was now time
to think about
his father's idea.
Sidney signed up
for a business course.
He also took
an English course.

On the first day,
Sidney had a surprise.
In walked
the new English teacher.

It was Mr. Fine!
Sidney had not seen
his friend
for years.
Not since Sol
had told Mr. Fine
to leave.

"I'm so happy
to see you,"
said Mr. Fine.
"How are you doing?"

Sidney told him
about the business course.

"That's very good,"
said Mr. Fine.
"I am sure
you would do well
in business."

Sidney did do well
in the business course.
He came away
with many ideas.

"I have been thinking,"
Sidney told his father.
"Let's start our factory
when I finish school.
We will make
the best shoes.
And we will make
more of them
than anyone else!"

"That's my boy!"
said Sol.
"Hard work
and long hours
make dreams come true
in America!"

But Sidney
also enjoyed
his English course.
He did not tell Sol
who the teacher was.
But he spent
many hours
writing papers
for Mr. Fine's class.

He learned
that he loved to write.

"You are very good,"
Mr. Fine told Sidney.
"You should think
about writing for a living."

"Not me,"
said Sidney.
"My father and I
plan to start
a shoe factory."

"Is this
what you want to do
with your life?"
Mr. Fine asked.

"Of course,"
said Sidney.

"Will you
follow the old ways
of being a Jew?"
asked Mr. Fine.

"I don't think so,"
said Sidney.
"I stopped going to temple
about a year ago.
Do you still meet
with those Jewish friends
of yours?"

"Yes,"
said Mr. Fine.
"Now I don't want
to get you into trouble.
But you are welcome
to come along with me."

"I'd like that,"
said Sidney.

The next Monday
a woman
came into the shoe shop.
"I saw your son
at the library,"
she said.
"He was with that man
who used to be your boarder."

Sol asked Sidney about it
that night.

"No, Papa,"
said Sidney.
"I was not
with Mr. Fine."

"You lie to me!"
said Sol.
"I won't have it!
I told that man
to never talk to you again!
First you start
going to coffeehouses
on Friday nights.
Then you stop
coming to temple
with me.
And now you lie
about seeing Mr. Fine.
That is enough!
Find yourself
another place to live!
You are not my son!"

Thinking It Over

1. What does Sol mean
   when he says,
   "You are not my son!"?

2. Do you think
   Sol got too angry?

3. Do you think
   a parent should ever
   kick a child
   out of the house?

4. What do you think will happen
   to the factory idea?

CHAPTER 10

Sidney found
a little room
near City College.
He got
a part-time job
in an office.
He needed
the money.
He didn't work
for his father anymore.

But Sidney
kept on taking
business courses.
He kept on thinking
things would get better.
Someday he and his father
would start their factory.
But he never heard
from his father.

Sidney still saw
Mr. Fine.
His friend and teacher
helped him
with his writing.
More than anything,
Sidney enjoyed writing.

One day
he met Emma
for dinner.

"How's Papa?"
he asked her.

"He is starting
the shoe factory,"
said Emma.
"He says
he must do it himself.
He says
he has no son."

"I think
the factory
should be on the East Side,"

said Sidney.
"That way,
it will be close
to the river.
Someday,
he can ship shoes
out of New York."

"I'll tell him,"
laughed Emma.

Then Sidney
pulled out
a thick pile of paper.
"I wrote a play,"
he said.
"It's about a woman
who lost touch
with her parents.
Will you read it?"

"Sure,"
said Emma.
"Is there
a part in it
for me?"

"You are the star
of the play."
said Sidney.

Emma laughed.

"I mean it!"
said Sidney.
"I want you
to act
the lead part!"

Emma took
the play home.
In a few days
she got together
with Sidney again.

"It's a great play!"
she said.
"I showed it
to the man
who runs the theater.
He likes your play.
He wants
to put it on."

"Don't kid me!"
said Sidney.

But what Emma said
was true.
The theater
signed up the play
for its fall season.

Sidney watched
the actors
getting ready.

"Who is that pretty woma
with the brown hair?"
he asked Emma.

"That's Helen Little,"
Emma told him.
"Do you want
to meet her?
She's not Jewish."

"I want
to meet her,"
Sidney said.

Thinking It Over

1. How do you hear
   about people you don't see?

2. If you wrote
   a play or book,
   what would it be about?

3. Would you go out
   with someone
   of a different religion?

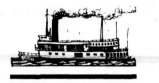

CHAPTER 11

Sidney and Helen
hit it off.
They went out
every night
after the play.

Sol never came
to see the play.
Sidney wrote it.
Emma acted in it.
But Sol never saw it.

Sidney met Emma
for dinner
once a week.
He wanted
to see his sister.
But he also cared
about his parents.
He wanted
to hear about them.

Sol put his factory
in a building
on the East Side
near the river.

"How's the shoe business?"
Sidney asked Emma.

"Papa knows
how to make shoes,"
Emma began.
"And he knows
how to sell them.
But he doesn't have
enough time
to do both."

"Tell him
to get outside sales people,"
said Sidney.

That's how
it went
week after week.
Sidney would give Emma
an idea.

She would carry it
back to Sol.
Sol would do
just what Sidney said.

Emma took home
other news, too.
Sidney and Helen
had decided to marry.
Sol and Hannah
were not happy.
Helen was not Jewish.
This made Sol
even more angry
with Sidney.
Emma and Hannah
went to the wedding.
Sol did not.

After the wedding
Helen came along
to dinners with Emma.
The three of them
were best friends.
They always had
a good time together.

Helen, too,
had good ideas
for Sol's shoe business.
Emma still told Sol
the new ideas.
His business grew.

But one night
Emma looked very sad.
Her eyes
were red.
She had been crying.

"What's the matter?"
Helen asked.

"I have
very bad news,"
said Emma.
"Papa is not well.
The doctor says
he does not have
long to live."

"I must see him,"
said Sidney.

"I can't
let him die
without talking
to him."

Emma told Sol
what Sidney had said.

"I don't have
a son,"
said Sol.

"Oh, come now,"
Hannah said.
"You do
have a son.
And he wants very much
to see his father."

Thinking It Over

1. Would you go
   to a wedding
   you did not believe in?

2. Why does it
   sometimes take bad news
   to get people together?

CHAPTER **12**

Sidney tapped
on the door.
"It's me,"
he said.
"Please let me in."

His mother
opened the door.
She put her arms
around Sidney's neck.

"Your father
is in the back room,"
she said softly.

Sidney walked
into the room.
"Papa?"
he said.

Sol looked up
from his bed.
"Has my son
come home?"
he asked.

"I have come
to see you,"
said Sidney.
"I am married now.
I live
with my wife."

"Have you changed
your ways?"
said Sol.

"Please, Papa,"
said Sidney.
There were tears
in his eyes.
It was hard
to speak.
"Don't be angry.
I have not gone back
to the old ways

of being Jewish.
But I am not
a bad person."

"You and I,
we built
our shoe factory,"
said Sol.

Sidney started
to talk.
Sol broke in.

"You know
this is true,"
Sol went on.
"You went to school
and learned
all about business.
You told Emma
your good ideas.
I listened
to everything
she told me
you had said."

"I guess
you are right,"
said Sidney.
"We built the business
together."

"Come here, my son,"
said Sol.

Sidney sat down
on the bed
near his father.

"I hope
you can forgive me,"
said Sol.
"I always loved you.
But my pride
made me treat you
the way I did."

Sidney reached out
and held Sol's hand.
"I love you, Papa,"
he said.

"Now what will happen
when I die?"
Sol asked
in a very soft voice.
"Who will carry on?"

"If you want me to,
I will take care
of the business,"
said Sidney.

Sol smiled.
"In one way or another
my dream will come true,"
he said.
"The business
is yours."

Sol closed his eyes.
He never woke up.

Thinking It Over

1. Have you ever
   had a dream come true
   in a way
   you had not planned?

2. What do you believe
   makes a dream come true?

3. Have you ever
   made peace with someone
   before they died?

CHAPTER 13

Sidney took over
the business.
He was surprised
at how much
he enjoyed
running the factory.
At last,
he could put to use
all his good ideas.

Sidney and Helen
made the business
grow very large.
They made lots of money.
They bought
a big house
on Long Island.
They had
three children.
They asked Hannah
to move in.

Emma married the man
who ran the theater.
They lived in the city.
But they often visited
the house on Long Island.

One day,
Sidney said to Helen,
"We don't have
enough time together.
Let's go away
for the weekend.
Just the two of us.
Mother can watch
the children."

So Sidney and Helen
drove up the coast.
They stopped
at a big hotel
by the ocean.

Sidney went inside.
He waited
at the front desk.
No one spoke to him.

He rang the bell
on the desk.
"I have been waiting,"
he told the man
behind the desk.
"May I please
have a room?"

"We have
no rooms left,"
said the man.

"What do you mean?"
asked Sidney.
"I saw you
give a key
to that other family.
You'll have to give me
a better reason."

"The reason is
who you are,"
said the man.

"Jewish, you mean?"
cried Sidney.

"Let me tell you something.
My grandfather
came to America
to be free.
My father
worked his fingers
to the bone
in this country.
I run
a big shoe factory
in New York.
I have the right
to stay anywhere
I want to!"

"Your kind of people
are not welcome here,"
said the man.
And he walked away.

Sidney could not believe
what was happening.
This man was telling him
that America
was *not* a free country
for Jews.

Sidney grew angry.
America was *not* Russia.
Jews should be as free
as any other Americans!

Then and there
Sidney made up his mind.
He would work
for the rights of Jews.
He would write and talk
and raise money.
He would help
other Americans
be fair to Jews.

Sidney walked
back to the car.

"I just learned something
about myself,"
he told Helen.
"I am Jewish.
I *really* am Jewish."

"You knew that,"
said Helen.

"But maybe
I never understood it,"
said Sidney.
"I can't be
like my father.
I can't be
that kind of Jew.
But my blood
is Jewish.
Nothing will ever change that.
And I don't want it to change.
I learned a lot
from my father.
I learned
how to work hard
and be fair.
And Mr. Fine showed me
how to be Jewish
in today's world.
From all of this,
I became Sidney Gold—
Jew,
American,
Person.
I must be free
to be all three."

Thinking It Over

1. What is your idea
   of being well off?

2. Do you believe
   that hotels or clubs
   should be closed
   to some people?

3. What people
   mean the most
   in your life?

4. What is most important
   to you—
   your country,
   your religion,
   your personal life, or—
   the right to go your own